Thank you f,
the time to , ..
I hope you enjoy it!

MW00579632

Oh...

THE LIVES WE LIVE

A NOVEL

Instagram
Jellz_b84
Jasminebrown0328@gmail.com
617-304-6365

THE LIVES WE LIVE

A NOVEL

JASMIN BROWN

JB Book Publishing
Stoughton, Massachusetts

Oh The Lives We Live
Published by:
JB Books
Stoughton, MA
Email: jasminebrown0238@gmail.com

Jasmin Brown, Publisher / Editorial Director
Yvonne Rose/Quality Press, Book Packager
Cover Photo by: Jayanii Brown

ALL CHARACTERS IN THIS BOOK ARE FICTIONAL

JB Books are available at special discounts for bulk purchases, sales promotions, fund raising or educational purposes.

DEDICATION

I dedicate this book to my Parents Kenneth and Vickie Brown.

I couldn't have thanked God enough for the parents He has blessed me with. You are the epitome of what real love is. I know daily how much you've sacrificed for me as your daughter and I am truly grateful to you guys. Each of you is a role model to me for different reasons.

My Mother is a powerful Pilar of strength with every obstacle that has been given to her. My Father is a Courageous Herculean who continues to protect me and my children's hearts. You guys always make sure that I remain safe, healthy and secure and I always appreciate you guys for that.

I have you two to thank for the way I turned out: Strong-willed and passionate. The two of you are forces to be reckoned with, and I adore your kindness, your fire and your compassion. Thank you for continuing to believe in me. I Love you.

ACKNOWLEDGEMENTS

To my Family. Thank you for supporting me and keeping me focused.

To my Girls, Victoria and Jayanii. I thank God that he chose me to be your mother. I love you.

To my other half, Kei. Thank you for always being there for me and continuing to encourage me.

To my Sister, Kenya The Originator. You are inspiring and an amazing writer I hope I made you proud.

Wake up from Dreaming and live your life !!!!

TABLE OF CONTENTS

Jasmin Brown

EDIRA

Oh the lives we live! *She exhaled a deep breath.* Here I am cuddling with Bae. Altogether our 6 hands intertwined like a web. Yes, I love him, he loves me, she loves him, and I love… well… just love him. You see my life has totally changed from what it used to be and I'm ok with it, right? My man Eric has expressed many times that he has so much of his self to give; and I thought I was in agreeance with him because I was in love.

So, here we are laying on the California style bed with Toni...Toni who they referred to in high school as "Tonka T". She's a pretty light brown girl with curly hair and a body that most women would pay for, I mean if I had the money. Wait, what am I saying? I can afford it, but I have more pressing things to worry about, thank you.

Toni got out of bed with her infamous booty shorts on that distract Eric from me when I'm having a heart to heart about how I tripped over the box at the office and landed face-first into the new printer machine. I mean, seriously, I dropped the best tea I had made in weeks and I think I skinned my shin to the white meat. But nonetheless, she has continued to captivate him with her vivacious curves and flexible limbs… bendy Bitch!

"Hey guys, would you like something to eat? I have some vegan eggs and some spinach. I can whip together a quick breakfast for you before I head to work".

We say "no thank you" in unison. I say, "I'll grab something healthy (A bacon egg with cheese on a bagel) on the way to work." Edira smiled and headed into the bathroom to take a shower. He we are, going on 2 years with this girl; and as much as I adore him and want him to be happy, is this really what I want? I look at affirmations on the mirror as I step out of the shower that says "Edira, you are amazing! Edira, you are Strong! Edira, all things we manifest will be positive Because you are Enough!"

EDIRA

Let's go back in time when it was just Eric and me. Ok BT, before Toni, of course. We started dating in college and became a couple shortly after. We would go to the movies and then out to eat and then, of course, head to the dorm room and rumble in the sheets. I call Eric E.T because we got that Extraterrestrial Thang going on in the bedroom. Hey, it's out of this world. After we graduated, he started his career as an IT engineer, and I became the assistant director for one of the top Fortune 400 Companies in the world.

It's crazy how I got the position I didn't even apply for initially. A friend of mine told me about the company and its core goals and values and, of course, its 401k and retirement plan was cool too. I walked into the office with my resume and cover letter wearing a suit I luckily found on the rack in the Department store and it was on sale. I love a bargain, OK! The woman who interviewed me was a tough cookie; but I could see right through that thick over-used makeup. I had this in the bag. Not only did I get a better   position I got my own office and parking spot… yyyaasss… #Winning #Blackgirlsrock.

A year and half later we're closing on our 3-bedroom, 2 bath home in a comfy location close to both our jobs. We would leave together in the morning smelling like fresh love-making and he would meet me for dinner after he got back from the gym. He was a health buff; he would work out for hours which would explain that flip move he did to me that almost took out the curtains and my back in the dining room. I loved the time we spent together it was beautiful and it was romantic, and we were fulfilled… or so I thought.

One late night of Netflix he started rubbing my feet and casually asked how I feel about bringing someone else into the bedroom. My face must have said it all, but I brushed it off as a joke and said sure they can change the room around. I'm not a fan of seeing our neighbor Gertrude the nudist, who can't seem to figure out how to close her curtains, especially while she's on the treadmill. I mean… come on lady. But no, he was serious. I told him to let me sleep on it and I'll let you know in the morning. During the course of our relationship, he would always bring up how another woman would be a perk for us and a great asset for him… he really meant the later.

A week later, we were in the café we frequent down the street, going thru profiles of women interested in a throuple. We scrolled past some cute ones, not so cute, big, little and even pint size. I really didn't have a preference because I didn't like women; but I also needed to make sure she wasn't as cute as me. I mean I wasn't bad looking at all - 5'4, dang it 5'3 – hey, my doctor said I can dream. Brown skin, a descent handful of booty and a lot of boobs which my ancestors have cursed me. But I was definitely beautiful and had a dope soul.

We decided to meet 5 women from the site so it would be one date a day and we spared the weekend so we could negotiate. So here we are, date number 1. Courtney was tall like Eric he's 6'2; she was about 5'9, so I was already annoyed. She could possibly take me down, man. What the hell? Next please. Date number 2 - Britnae with an "e", not a Y - came in like something stank; and yes, it was her attitude. Girl, bye. At this point, I'm feeling like maybe this isn't such a good idea, we need someone more… well, like you know… me. So, here we are at Date number 3, Maria. She came in with the shoes that Monica had on in the "Before you walked out my life" video. And with that, Maria's date was so gone, hey! She should've known better. Date 4, Jessica. At first sight, she was not bad-looking. She had pretty hair and was well put together. We hit it off in the beginning. *Notice, I said "the beginning".* We all had a drink or two, but Miss Jessica was throwing them back like it was shortage in the restaurant. And then it happened… she started balling, crying her eyes out and gagging. So now, you're making a scene in this lovely establishment - boogies and anything else you can imagine leaving from her face. I was officially done.

We left that place leaving a hefty tip and sending Jessica home in a Lyft, praying she got home safe. She posted a picture of her disheveled look on the gram… what a mess. I decided, *ok, this is the last date… so, no problem. We will get thru this and it will be all over with.* Hence, Date number 5 – Toni. My feeling was the first 4 were a bit much; but it's Friday and once this date is over we can continue on and not have to focus on this anymore.

Two years later…

ERIC

Oh, the lives we live … and trust me, I'm living it. You see I'm a Handsome Black man with a career that continues to push me to the next level of greatness, not to mention a ripped body that I've worked on since high school football, and I look like someone that fell out of an Essence magazine. I keep myself very well put together, I must say, and it shows - brown skin, full lips and "grabbing goatee". *Ladies love that shit.* So for me it was only right to be able to share this greatness with more than one lovely lady… right? I mean, I love Edira. She's sexy, beautiful and she's a boss on so many levels. But Man, listen. I'm also sexy, Beautiful and a Boss; so why not allow someone else to admire me.

Edira and I have been going strong for years. We have history and I appreciate her for holding me down when I had a job delivering pizza and accidently got caught up in scheme to cash app people and get them more money. That didn't go too well; but she still was there and helped me to be a better man and I am forever grateful for that. I had been

Jasmin Brown

mulling over this decision for some time and definitely wanted to be direct with Edira. I just knew if I was sneaky and cheated Edira wouldn't embarrass me like a ratchet chick, Edira would get back at me so skillfully I would be biting my nails until my nickname was num nums. But all jokes aside. I'm hoping that Edira is down for this. She's my rock we go together like peanut butter and jelly, I just want to be able to add some butter to my bread. You feel me? I have to come to the conclusion that I can make this work with two women. I can please both of them the way they need and provide whatever they desire; and in return, they will have to commit themselves to only me.

So here we are - date after date, one disappointing one after the next. One Girl was almost neck and neck with me. Nope, I'm cool. One reminded me of the rude ass cashier with the mustache at the convenience store who would be rolling her eyes to the back of her head. And the other chick came in with them, Monica kicked down your door and slapped your chick shoes. My eyes went straight to her feet. Shit, I hope she didn't take it personal. The fourth date started out great. We were vibing and having a good time; but then shit went south after she requested one too many Shots. My cut-off was 2. I'm a light drinker and Edira probably waited until her drink was watered down to even

8

finish. So I knew things were not looking too good once she had that 5th one down. This girl started crying and then I saw snots and drool, and that was it for me. I have a weak stomach. We were both about to be throwing up in this place. But lucky for her we managed to leave out of the establishment with a little bit of dignity and she made it home safely. Thank goodness for gram Notifications.

So, I was feeling like throwing in the towel, calling it quits; but we had one more date left. Hey, why not? We had a couple laughs - some gag worthy situations - and even a possible hospitalization. But I'm not a quitter. We had one more date to go on… so let's do it.

Man, when I tell you the chick walked into the door all I could hear was, "I want some of your brown sugar…ooohhh oohhhh". Baby girl had front, back, side to side. I didn't want to show my excitement, so I tried to remain calm. Edira, however, saw the glossy look I had and wiped the drool from my bottom lip real hard like an annoyed parent. She walks over to our table and introduces herself, and from that day she was the additive to my already healthy plate. We did everything together - we ate dinner, watched movies, and went on walks, and even to the bars and clubs.

It was my dream that was finally a reality. I could make love to Edira on Monday; get some Head from Toni on Tuesday; Wednesday is a toss-up of whichever is in the mood; Thursday, I'm bending someone over the Lazy Boy; Friday, someone is getting a special eat treat and I'll finish the rest of the weekend with who I choose. It's simple. I please them, they please me – separately, of course. They both are women with needs that I provide to them, individually. They always get "Me" time, so it works.

TONI

Oh, the lives we live … and yet I've never thought I would be in this kind of situation… but I guess it's intriguing. You see, I have never had an issue getting men. I attract them like good discounts, and yes everyone loves a banging sale. It's been like this for the longest time. I've been shapely since high school and it has only gotten better with time. I eat healthy, I work out, and I mediate every day. I have to keep this body in tune… they don't call me "Tonka T" for nothing. I got a hefty wagon I'm dragging with cute dimples on it too. I'm as natural as can get and I always seem to get a side-eye from some girl, like I'm the reason they ass looked like it was hit with a book bag. I got long beautiful hair with extra to spare. The crazy part is I'm not a hater, Women are beautiful. I'm not into to them; but, I can acknowledge a pretty chick and think, *ok bitch go head wit your bad self.*

As I said earlier, I frequent the gym quite often; so a couple of my friends from work meet me there so we can decompress from my intense schedule of being an ER

Nurse. I find my regular spot near the clean mats away from the bathroom; because Lucy the lady that works in the lunchroom always be in there stinking it up and acting like it was someone else. But I just mind my business and pay the hand that feeds me.

My friends, Chantel and Sonya, come dragging their asses into the gym with food and drinks, knowing damn well they ain't supposed to be eating in here. Chantel sits right in front of me on one of the yoga balls with a vanilla shake in her hand, asking me how long I've been in here. She thinks she can get away with it because she's sleeping with Terrance, the custodial Engineer aka Janitor. Sonya usually just comes as a plus one, because she's only interested in snatching up ancient men; she don't care who it is, she loves them senior citizens. I've had to break up many fights with old ladies behind Sonya's messing with these geriatric men. Canes and loose change are flying everywhere.

So, Chantel starts telling me how she's taking a break from Terrance because he told her he got new responsibilities at work and they gave him more hours. Even though I've seen Terrance talking to the thick chick that does the Pilates classes in the evening during those

"Extra Hours". So, for her, "more hours" mean less time and she don't have any of that to waste. She tells me about a new dating site that's been out for a while that has a dynamic of relationships that we might not consider but may think about. I asked her the name and she told me she'll send me the link.

I get home, hop in the shower, lather what feels like hours of tension and anxiety, rinse off, then get out. I put on some music and take out a fresh bowl of fruit that I got from the grocery store yesterday. I'm enjoying my jams, then decide to get on the site and see what's on there. I've always wanted to have a divergent relationship, but I just didn't know to what extent. The Main page is set up like a normal site with different relationship types in each corner. I click on the one that I'm interested in and begin my search.

I came across a couple of profiles; and then one stopped me in my tracks. Him. I've seen him before walking down my street heading into a coffee shop with a pretty brown chick. I was doing a load of laundry and happened to be changing my clothes over and I saw him. He was tall, chocolate, muscular; had a short fade, with the cutest dimples, a "grabbing goatee", and beautiful teeth. It was like he was moving in slow motion and he had on grey sweats that also were moving in slow motion. Yes, please!

Once I realized it was him in the photo, I immediately messaged him hoping I would get a response. Bingo, N39! He sent me a message the next day. Eric was his name and Edira was his lady's name. I was nervous as hell, as I got ready for the night; but I made sure all my physical attributes were highlighted. I walked into the restaurant and saw them sitting together. He looked so damn good. But why was she wiping his lip like my grandmother when I had crusty stuff on my face? I get to the table and he reintroduces himself and Edira. The conversation flowed so well and smooth and I just knew this was going to be the start of an amazing beginning for me... and an unfortunately and sad ending to this long act for Edira.

EDIRA

I find myself sometimes asking if this is really worth it. Here it is, I've spent my prime waiting for this man to want to settle down and marry me, then maybe bring some babies into this world; but now I'm in my late thirties sharing my time and man with this young girl who could probably get her own. So, I've been thinking a lot about if it may be time to move on from this. My heart says *you love him he loves you; you've been down for each other for forever*. But then my mind says, *why am I not good enough, why do you feel like you need another woman to give you what you want and desire?* I mean, to me, its extra work for him. Please two women, deal with two periods, and let alone feed two women that don't have the same taste at all. I mean, "hello! Taco Bell has salad, to bitch, get a tortilla filled with lettuce."

Right now, I'm definitely giving a straight face and being polite and not trying to make anyone uncomfortable; but I definitely think that it's time to make some much-needed changes. I call my Best friend Jovi so he can come over and make me beautiful. Jovi has been my best friend since middle school and has been more like family. He has his own Hair and Nail salon called JV Naturals. Jovi also is an excellent stylist and can walk in heels better than most women I know. Jovi tells me he can come tomorrow to my house, unless I want to come into the shop; because he's convinced his cousin who works for him has been stealing hair products, but he just can't fire her because her design game is dope.

So I patiently wait for the next day. Hey, I can't be outside looking like my momma don't love me. Jovi shows up with hair and the best products for natural women. I told him I was interested in small box braids. I needed a style to last some time, and plus, I needed girl talk. Jovi starts in, already talking about my scalp. "Bitch what you been doing with my hair?" (I'm his hair crush). "You got my scalp looking dehydrated and thirsty, bitch Nurse!!! please, I need some moisturizer and maybe a little wine. I got work to do!!"

Jovi can always make me laugh, even though I haven't been feeling like myself lately. Jovi could tell and immediately started asking his usual. "So how's the Groupie? Have you decided to include Toni on your Eric days? Why did he choose her and not him? He's too much. I tell him no I'm not interested in her and am starting to lose interest in him as well. He almost choked on his wine when I said that. "What wait you're ready to give up ET so Toni can have him? Bitch, you lying!" Jovi rolls his eyes. "The way you said he used to do that thing with his mouth! Gggiiirrrlll, you can't let her keep him to herself. Pass him over to me."

A look of sadness came over my face and Jovi immediately came over and hugged me. "Edira, you are a dope bitch! Any man that can't see that needs a new prescription; you hear me?!" I thanked him because he knows me all too well and definitely can tell I've had my fill of this. I tell Jovi that I'm thinking about maybe making a drastic change, like cutting my hair or getting booty implants. He looked at me like I had completely lost it. He said, "girl give me your hair. I can make magic with this and it's your beauty that gets the good ones, never your booty darling".

He has me rolling sometimes with him. He finished my hair, which took about 4 hours and we sat for a while after that, just catching up with what's going on in his life. Jovi is doing a hair magazine and wants me to be one of his hair models. Of course I oblige. Why would I not want people to see all of this beautiful hair God blessed me with. He tells me he will give me the details once everything is finalized. I give him kisses and hugs and he heads home. I look at myself in the mirror and start posing like I've been modeling all my life. Jovi knows he can do some hair. I take a shower and lotion up really good and put on a big t shirt with no panties 'cause tonight is my night with Eric and soon he will be entertaining what lies between my brown-skin thighs.

I went to the bedroom and burned some incense, while drinking my tea that I had on the stove brewing and put on Silk's "Freak me baby". The intro started, I belted out "Let me lick you up and down till you say stop; let me play with your body, baby, make you real hot". I lay down in the bed awaiting Eric to come in bouncing that thing like it was on hydraulics. I woke up with my alarm blaring, dry sheets and no Eric in sight. *Where was he?*

ERIC

"She's a very freaky girl, don't bring her to momma. First, you get her name than you get her number." Shit…. "Damn girl, don't stop! Oh fuck… I'm about to… yo !! why you stop?" Eric I am not letting you cum in my mouth, I'm a lady. "I'm sorry, Tiana. But damn, girl, didn't your mother always tell you to finish your Popsicle and don't make a mess." We both laughed in unison. Tiana was a traffic stop waiting to happen.

I had just left from getting my car detailed and was changing the music on my Bluetooth and apparently I was taking too long at the stop sign and looking suspicious in the process because I saw the flashing lights. I kept my hands on the wheel and waited for whichever jerk was coming to my window harassing me as they always do. I've been pulled over so many times by these police, because I used to fuck the police chief's daughter and she started acting crazy over me and had her dad thinking I was playing her. I was, but that's not the point I was young, and I wasn't interested in being tied down. So now, every time they get behind me… sometimes, they'll just follow me or other times they'll find a reason to pull me over to give me a warning or a bogus ass ticket.

I heard a knock at the window and went to roll my window down. Good got damn! Tits for days, ass for weeks. "Excuse me sir, do you know why I pulled you over?"

"No ma'am, but I've definitely been a bad boy though," showing my pearly whites. She looked at me, smiled and said, "you've been sitting at this Stop sign for some time and it looked suspicious." I apologized and offered to take her out to eat. She was gorgeous. Carmel had long curly hair, and like I said earlier, "ass, ass ,ass, ass, ass ,ass." She told me that she would go out with me, but first I had to let her give me a ticket. She had 68 tickets and she wanted one more to make it 69. I told her "I'll let her give it to me just as long as I get my 69 worth." Man, I've been fucking her ever since. She finishes me off and I pass her a napkin to wipe her mouth. She meets me at my office parking garage for a little late night of head games. She was sucking me off so much I fell asleep in the Range and woke up pants down at about 2 am.

Damn!! This was Edira's night, she's going to kill me. I got home hopped in the shower and got right in my bed. I know at this point she wouldn't want me to mess with her, once Edira's asleep, don't fuck with her... she loves dream land. I had to figure out what I was going to tell her . My tire popped... no, she knows I just got new rims. I had to work late. Nope, I can take my work home with me... fuck it! Bubble guts it is. Just remember, Eric, when you go into the kitchen make sure to hold your belly and say you've been in pain all night and make sure you apologize and maybe send her some flowers to work... she loves that shit.

I stepped into the entrance. She was already in the kitchen area looking just as beautiful as the day I met her. "Good morning, Edira. You got your hair braided, you look like Brandy, baby, I wanna be down!!!" She looked at me, drank her tea and walked out right past me. Wait, what did I forget to do? "Oh shit! Hey baby, I'm sorry about last night I had the bubble guts real bad...would of cleared out the whole house. I'll make it up to you, I promise. You love me?" Made sure I gave her the puppy dog eyes for full effect. Edira looked at me and said, "it's cool luv, I'm just glad you're ok and she kissed me on the cheek and left for work." Yes, I'm saved. I did my "I'm still getting it" dance right now.

I have to figure out how I can introduce Tiana to my girls and vice versa, shit what's one more. My plan is to take the girls, set them up for a spa day, take them out to eat at our favorite restaurant; then when we get home… bam, I think daddy needs a new ride. Well, maybe I'll work out the best way to ask for another girlfriend without being a total ass; but hey, they'll get the gist of what I'm requesting. Hopefully, Tiana will be on board being lovely lady number three…don't worry there's plenty of me to go around. I got these woman wrapped around my finger. I'm sure they'll both give in to what I want, they love me and I I always give them what they want.

TONI

S hit!!! I'm going thru my bag trying to find the empty medicine container. Damn it! I've been dropping my Klonopin in Edira's tea for the last few weeks and I've suddenly run out. How can I get a new prescription for this, so that I can keep making her drowsy so Eric and I can have more time? I mean I love this man and would do anything for him, but I see how he looks at her. I'm sick and tired of playing like I want to continue to share him. News flash, "I don't!" Don't get me wrong. Edira is a cool ass chick very down to earth, and easy to talk to. I've spent numerous days picking her brain, getting advice from her and even spending a little time with her .

But I want him all to myself. I tried a few different things to get him to start focusing more on me. I've taken on his laundry and cooking; I walk out of the bathroom with just a towel on while he's conversing at the table with her; I go to the Gym with him, making sure I wear the most revealing leggings and bra set; and when I give him head, I even swallow… what the hell! I want her gone now.

Tomorrow, when I go to work I will sneak a prescription pad from the office and forge the doctor's name and get something heavier that'll have her sleeping for days. Night night, Edira.

I went into work and was able to retrieve the pad and looked thru the meds that the doctor prescribed for difficulty sleeping. I dropped off the prescription at the pharmacy and waited in the car for it to be filled. I watched a couple of videos of "Snapped" and "First 48" because those are my two favorite shows. I paid attention to what the people did wrong that got caught and thought to myself, *that will never be me, I wouldn't be that dumb*. Wait! Am I turning into a crazy person over this man? It can't be I just love him so much and want him to leave Edira's meat eating, incense stinking, always wants the last word alone. Is that a lot to ask for?

I'm heading home in the car, reminiscing about the recent time Eric came into the shower, bent me over and entered me like I was the first and last thing on his mind. He pulled my hair and slapped my ass and told me that it belonged to him. I felt myself getting wet in the car. I had to get home, I know today is a toss-up of who gets Eric; but I'll be making sure it's me tonight. Whatever I have to do to make him see that "we belong together" as Mariah Carey plays on my Sirius XM station. I was determined and damn near ready to give Edira her eviction notice.

Maybe I could start discussing how Eric makes love to me and how he's always telling me how good it is. But then, I remember Edira will probably slap you off the side of the breakfast nook with her Ham and cheese still in hand. Ewww... gross... I hate meat. But Eric's meat I love. I love the fitted boxers he wears when walking around the house, I love when he rocks the basketball shorts and that thing be swinging. "Hit me with your best shot... ooowwww." My bad. I changed the station by accident, but still a banger!!! Eric knows exactly how I feel about him, and I've been patient with him, hoping he'll just say Toni T you are the only woman for me. "No No No you don't love me, and I know nooowwww." Damn it, with the radio acting up again.

EDIRA

"**M**s. Edira, you have a phone call. Ms. Edira, you have a phone call should I put her thru? Ms. Edira, is everything ok?" I looked up at my Assistant and apologized I didn't understand why I was feeling so tired. "You can put the call thru Angela, thank you". "Hello how are you, Cindy. I'm well… yes, I would like to set up an appointment to view the properties you found. I love that area, it's beautiful. I would definitely prefer the gated community… I like the extra security. Thank you, I will be in touch."

I had spoken to my real estate agent about a few different condos and some townhouses, and had made plans to go look at a home about 30 minutes away from my job and possibly an additional 10 from the house I share with Eric and Tanky… I mean Toni. It was a nice cul-de-sac and had about four houses on the street, which is great because I love my privacy. I had been getting this strange feeling about Toni and it hadn't been sitting well with me; and the fact that I haven't been spending much time with Eric hasn't really been bringing us close together either.

Jovi called me and asked if he can take the pictures of me this weekend for the magazine. I told him yes. I just needed to view a couple of places, then after that I was all his. I pulled up to the 2-story home where Cindy and I were to meet, it was on a nice quiet street with amazing houses and beautiful yards… or so I thought. As soon as I walked to the front door, a car with spinning rims (I didn't know they still made those) screeches up to the house next to the one I was viewing, and a dude with a baggy doo-rag with jeans tighter than braids that have you up all night fast-walking across the front lawn. "Patrice!!! Bitch, I know you're home! I called you 8 times and you keep sending me to voice mail. You know I love your dumb ass. Why you come to my job talking about I gave you the clap? I was about to get a promotion!!" I jumped back in my car and called up Cindy and told her to meet me at the next house, but not before Patrice came outside with a Pitbull the size of a small horse and let him loose on doo-rag. I had never seen a man jump so high in my life. "Bitch, get Tiny! Why you let that nigga out? You know he don't like me!!" That was the latest episode of when niggas ain't shit, tune in next time.

TIANA

Oh, the lives we live. This dude, Eric, got me hooked. I met him during a traffic stop. I've been trying to get back on track since my divorce and am focusing on being a better me. Xavier and I were high school sweethearts, but it's been a tumultuous relationship from the jump. Xavier would have women calling my phone talking shit to me and had to snatch a few bitches in behind him. One day I went by his mother's house, but she wasn't there. It was his rude-ass aunt, Trina, the one who can't never keep her mouth or legs closed. Why did his aunt feel the need to start talking shit to me to get me out the house? He must of heard the commotion and came out with just boxers on and the girl was right behind him with her bra and his shorts on. I lost it. His aunt's baked beans and mac and cheese were all over the floor, after I got done with that chick.

I dragged her from the bedroom thru the kitchen and out the front door. I stepped on their dog. Chino, who was 13 years old and had cataracts... sorry Chino, my bad.

Needless to say Xavier and I were not the perfect match; but yet I still gave him another chance because I loved him. We were going strong for a while and then I found out I was pregnant. He was so happy and wanted to get married. He told me he didn't want his child to be without his dad and he wanted both of us to have his last name. We planned a small intimate wedding and it was beautiful. Three months into our marriage, I lost the baby.

It went downhill from there. He became abusive and blamed me for the loss. He would come home pissy drunk and said he despised the look of me because I couldn't keep our baby alive. The last straw for me was when I was asleep and slapped out of my slumber. I rolled out of bed and wiped my mouth. I saw blood and then I saw red. I don't remember much of anything, I completely blacked out. I threw anything and everything I could get my hands on. The house phone, the iron, my sock of rocks I got from my dad… he always told me to use it as a weapon for anyone who would try me.

I think once the fight was over Xavier left my house looking like the X-men… I took out at least 3 of his interview teeth. As the medics took him out I told him you've done enough to me and I will never let a man do that to me, ever again. So I joined the Police force and became a cop to protect myself and serve a nigga a necessary ass-whooping. So, when Eric and I became a couple, I was scared because I was falling for him fast and hard. He would come to my house and we'd do it everywhere. There wasn't one spot in my house that was untouched by our body sweat. We even, from time to time, did it in his Range Rover or sometimes my squad car. Whoop whoop… that's the sound of the police.

I began to wonder why we never did it at his place; but he told me that he was building one from the ground up and that's why we got expensive hotel rooms. I began to feel like he might be keeping something from me, but I didn't know what and why; so, I brushed it off until I felt like I needed to contact Irving down in records to pull some information for me. Irving got a thing for me. He also got a dry Jheri Curl that's never activated and a questionable gold tooth, but that's beside the point. He can be quite helpful with some light flirting and perfume.

I'm content with how our relationship is going and continued to enjoy the time we spent together. I hope this will last forever… I hope you're the man of my dreams Eric.

EDIRA

I sat in my car a little later than normal, feeling sick to my stomach. What the hell was going on with me? I had a headache, and I had to pee every 6 steps and was extremely tired. Did I have a UTI? I decided to take the day off and get some rest at home, but not before stopping at the drug store to get my chocolate and salt and vinegar chips. I knew that my period was due any day now and I just wanted to be prepared. I get in line to pay for my stuff and I see Toni at the drive thru with a scarf and glasses on, like she was trying to be incognito. That girl is way past Looney Tunes, but whatever... dam it, I forgot to grab some cranberry juice and my root beer... I like the burp. I get out the line and go past the woman's health section. Something tells me to grab a pregnancy test. I'm not sure why, because it had been a while since Eric and I had done the do.

But I remember the day he was supposed to be there, and he wasn't... he definitely made it up the next night. I was in the bedroom writing in my Self-Love Journal. I put the pen down in the journal and sat it on my nightstand. I hit the lights and then I felt him. He was lifting the back of my t-shirt up to kiss the lower part of my back. Of course, I was annoyed; but then, I remembered the 3-dozen flowers he sent to my office. The card read "With Love from ET, you already know…." And yes, I did!!!! He wrapped his hand underneath my shirt to squeeze my boob and started biting my ear." Let me taste some of that sweet shit".

You ain't got to ask me but once. He flipped me over and started kissing my stomach slow and steady, he likes to take his time. Then he opened my legs and dived in head first into that honey pot. From time to time he would look up at me and wink… he loved the way I tasted. After I came for the third time. He came back up and slid right in. He started telling me how much he loves me how good it is and that it belongs to him. Eric then put me in Doggy style which he knows is my shit because I'm a Nasty Bitch, apparently in heat.

If you see two lines, it's positive. I kept looking at the box and looking at the test, looking at the box and back at the test. Is this for real? No, I'm bugging and that's why I bought the 2-pack. Let's try this again. 5 minutes on the clock. I selfishly looked over in 3 minutes. Two of the darkest pink lines I've ever seen. What! Oh my goodness, This can't be! How, when, why? I know the answers. I just wasn't ready to accept them. So here I am in the bathroom, alone with two very positive tests in hand. I place them down, wash my hands, and dry them with the embroidered hand towel I got from my Godmother.

I go to throw the box in the trash and noticed that there was already a pregnancy test thrown away. Wait I know I only bought one box so…. Oh my goodness I sat back down on the edge of the tub. Could Toni possibly be pregnant too? My mind is going in a million different directions now. He told me they use protection; he was only nasty with me. And wait he has condoms everywhere in this house. What is he doing, using them for decorations? I said to myself, *please give me the strength to figure this shit out and not need to strangle someone.*

I called my doctor to make an appointment and see when I could get in. She gave a time for that Monday and I put it in my phone to set as a reminder. Now, what do I do? Should I tell Eric that I'm expecting, or should I ask him about the pregnancy test I already found that technically wasn't mine. Eric and I have been together for a while, maybe this is how things will come together. Maybe this is telling me to give him another chance.

TONI

This cannot be happening! This can't be! What the fuck is going on? I had been thinking about the test that I took last week and how I didn't want to be in this situation again. Eric and I had gotten pregnant a few months ago and I decided to abort it because I wasn't ready to be a mother. I never told him, just kinda kept my distance after I got the procedure due to the bleeding. I was contemplating birth control, but I didn't like the way it made my body feel when I was a teenager, so I opted out. Now, here I am pregnant again, extremely emotional and wanting to cry every 5 minutes.

I knew something was up with me when I watched that insurance commercial and started balling my eyes out "Grandpa always going to be there, Hailey, he is." But maybe this was a sign, Toni. Maybe this would be a way to get Eric to leave Edira alone and just be with me. But Edira is such a good person, Toni, She could help you with the baby, she does have mothering instincts. Shut up Toni! you got this you don't need no help, just Eric by your side.

I go to the Pharmacy and pick up the prescription to help my friend Edira get some much-needed rest so I can tell Eric our good news. I'm in the Drive-thru with my grandma's head scarf and some glasses I took at lost-and-found in the gym. I figured I was going to dine him and wine him, maybe even 69 him, and then tell Eric the news. I'm going to wait until the weekend is over to let him know he's going to be a daddy. So, my plan was to make it a memorable Monday to remember. I would prepare, I mean purchase his favorite meal. I unfortunately fell short when I started preparing dinner. I would put on the sheer nighty he bought me from the lingerie store and put on that TlC Red light special jam.

We would eat dinner together as we always do and I would offer to make Edira some tea to help her get some much-needed rest, of course. I've noticed she's been complaining of back problems and has been in a mood; but then again, Edira your boobs are big ass shit, so, whatever …not my problem. She's been a pain since the day I met her and I'm so over seeing them together.

I look at myself in the mirror and decide to call this number called JV Naturals to make an appointment. I heard he does the bomb roller-set. Sunday evening, I go to his salon. He was playing Lil Kim "Dreams". The dude was mad cool and very funny and I felt like I was in a therapy session. I told him about what I did for a job and how I was in a relationship with a man and another woman. He noticed that I came with crackers and ginger ale and I told him I just recently found out I was expecting. He seemed very interested, at this point, asking if I told my boyfriend or the other woman. I told him I was going to surprise my man and was hoping that the other woman would just leave us be. I showed him a picture of Eric and me, and he said I had good taste. I thanked him and he asked me more about why I didn't want the other women to still be involved. I told him "I understand she came before me, but I'm the better catch, and that I would do anything in my power to get rid of her!!!"

It was crazy because once I said that he kind of bopped me on the head with his metal comb and then apologized because he said he had greasy hands. So, he finally finished up and of course I looked dope. I gave him a tip and he gave me one too. He told me what happens in the dark always comes to light. Honey, just be honest with them both. I thanked him and left thinking, *yeah, ok... that's not going to happen. I'm going to continue to do what I've been doing, boo, and won't anyone stop me.* I'm ready for what's yet to come and I'm looking forward to what Eric and my future holds.

EDIRA

"Hello. Good afternoon, Doctor Stevens. I'm doing ok, sure I can come in. Is everything alright? Ok, no problem… see you at 2". I'm not sure why my doctor is calling me and asking me to come in. I hope everything is ok with the baby… I was just there this morning. I go in the obstetrics office and sit down in the waiting room, waiting for my name to be called. I noticed my doctor's office had a lot of African Artifacts on her walls and a nice little selection of magazines and books. I picked up one of the books with a woman with an amazing Afro on the cover. The book read "Open" by Kenya Brown Milfort. Why have I seen this before? Oh yeah, when I'm sitting in my car I've seen this book plastered on a billboard in the city. She must be doing big things. I look at the Television and she's interviewing with Tyler Perry, discussing how they have just finished up the Movie and how it will be out in theaters soon. Go head, girl, I see you!!!

The Nurse called me and brought me into the office. I was a little confused, normally I go into an exam room…

but ok. Doctor Stevens is a heavy-set pretty Black woman with beautiful short hair, and she wears her glasses on her nose. I came in and sat down and she looked at me over her glasses and asked "how long have you been taking Ambien?" I looked puzzled, dam near confused. Ambien? Why would I be taking Ambien? My doctor explains that Ambien is for Chronic Insomnia and can be used for Depression as well.

I know I've been off lately, but I just assumed it was because of the pregnancy. I assured Doctor Stevens that this must be a mistake. She shows me my chart and shows me my levels, and then I'm even more baffled. I tell her all I've been drinking has been my tea at home and maybe some apple juice that I bring to work.

"Are you sure you haven't just, maybe by accident, been taking someone else's medicine?" Now you're just being ignorant. "No Doctor Stevens, I have not". Then I stop and think. Wait! Is it possible that someone is putting shit in my drink at work? It must be Susie. She's had a hit out for me since she found out I was the one given the position she applied for. I'm sorry, Susie, that you come into work late most times and always look like you were on a secret rendezvous.

Nonetheless, I told her I will make sure to take my prenatal and get to the bottom of what's going on. She brings me into the exam room and checks the baby. It's moving around and kind of just looks like a blob but I'm still happy to see it. She prints out the pics and I head to the store to grab some things because I planned on spending the rest of the day with Jovi. He had been calling me checking on me a lot today, and I thought it was quite sweet and a little strange. I get to Jovi's house and buzz his door. He lets me up to his apartment it's the cutest little place, everything is gold and black from the countertops to the rugs.

Over in the Corner on his gold bed was Minaj, his Miniature Maltese. He had just finished up some booty length singles and baby girl was swinging it. She was in Jovi's floor length mirror, twerking and talking about she going to make them drop them dollars. He was dancing with her saying "yyyyyaaassss pop it and drop it bitch." She pays Jovi and heads for the door, not without slightly hitting me with her braids on the way out... the audacity. I sit down on his black leather couch and proceed to eat the crackers I got from the store. Jovi comes over and gives me a long and loving hug, like he hadn't seen me in years. I ask him is everything alright? He says, "girl I know you're sitting, but you about to be laid the fuck out after I tell you what happened last night."

I fake fall out and pick myself up like I'm in class ready to get a lesson." BBBBiiiittttccchhh, you will never guess whose hair I did, and chick was straight off her rocker!!" I paused… I didn't know who he could possibly be talking about. "Bitch, your Nigga's other Chick, Toni Mutha fuckin T". I froze. *How would he have known it was her and why would she come to him?* bitch said she don't trust no one with her hair but herself. I say to Jovi, "continue." He goes on to say they were having really good conversation until shit got personal. I looked puzzled. "Personal like what?" He said they started talking about her throuple and that she planned on getting rid of the third wheel. He then says "did you know that hoe was pregnant?" I looked away. Of course I knew, I saw the box in the dam trash; but, to hear it from Jovi just solidified that she was, in fact, expecting too. So, he continues on to say, "be careful she reminds me of them crazy chicks on snap, like, she has more than just a simple plan to remove you from this equation." He sips invisible Tea.

Then I paused. Wait a minute. Is this why she has been acting so nice and sweet and offering to prepare my lunch and make me tea certain nights. *Oh my God, it's Toni! Toni has been putting the medicine in my cup. That conniving little bitch.* I hugged Jovi and told him that I loved him and that I had something to handle. I grab my stuff and tell him "if I call you from jail just make sure you got bail" and ran out. I headed to the house. I was going to beat the shit out of her. How dare she put my unborn child's life in danger over some man! Is she crazy? Oh yeah, she cooked alright and she about to get a cast iron pan to the head.

I arrive to the house and sit in the car for a minute. I think about everything that has transpired over the last several weeks and what I can possibly lose. I turned off the radio and said a prayer. I asked God for forgiveness and for clarity. I then asked God that if I get time that my baby will be ok. I turn the radio back on and Brooke Valentine "It's about to be a girl fight" blast out the radio. Let's go bitch!

What transpired in that house will forever change my life and not how you could imagine.

ERIC

I'm at the Bar, drinking with my boy Reggie, watching the football game. My team is being destroyed right now, but I keep my cool because Reggie is a cocky-ass nigga. Reggie has been one of my road dogs for a long time and always tells me I'm the shit because I got 2 sets of hands, 2 mouths, and 2 cats at my discretion, not to mention the new chick I've been piping down. Reggie's talking mad shit now cause his team is up by 6. "Nigga why you mad? You mad? Don't be mad. You need a hug? Call your tribe, nigga… and he burst out laughing.

He annoys me sometimes because, for me, it's just a game; but he be acting like his life is going to end if his team loses. I try to brush it off, but he keeps bringing up my girls. Like they don't have anything to do with this conversation, nigga. He just mad 'cause I can say "look ma no hands" 'cause I got three playing with my dick, nigga. "Yeah yeah, your team is winning good for you, nigga. Collect your coins, pass go and collect 200 bucks". "He said, "whatever nigga, I want my chips with dip bitch."

"Now hold on nigga, you know calling another man a bitch is a violation. Please don't make me embarrass you in front of these people." Reggie calms down. He remembered that I used to save him from a lot of ass-whooping in school. Even dudes smaller than him, he know he can't fight. I decide to call it a night and finish watching the game in the comfort of my home with my girls. He asks if he can tag along. I tell him, "don't be acting stupid in my house or you'll get put the fuck out." He throws his hands up in submission. I tell him we going in his whip 'cause he just bought a new Benz and I wanted to see how it drove too… maybe add to my collection of possessions.

We get to the house and go inside, and Toni has those soft curls I love and got on the nighty I got her from the lingerie store. I told her to take her ass upstairs and put on a robe. She looks at me with her face looking sad and her lip poked out and saunters upstairs. I can feel Reggie's eyes watching my girl's ass, as she walks up the steps. I cut him a look and he quickly says. "my bad" and he sits down, and I grab us some drinks out the fridge. The game is on not even 10 minutes I hear the front door open and slam, I look up and see rage in Edira's eyes. I definitely didn't think my life was about to change.

Oh the lives we lived.........

Edira came into the house and didn't say a word to either of us. She started screaming at the top of her lungs, "where the fuck is that bitch Toni!" Reggie and I jump up off the couch and look at her like she was a crazy woman. I yelled, "what's going on? Why are you acting like that?" She looks me dead in my face and says, "so you decided that Toni would be the better mother than me... is that it?" I looked confused. "What?" What the fuck are you talking about, Edira?" She said it one more time, but with a lot more tone and volume. At this point, Toni is rushing down the stairs with a robe that barely closed hollering, "who you calling a Bitch, Edira? I will beat your old ass in this kitchen". The girls are face to face at this point and I'm in the middle.

Did I turn around and this nigga Reggie is recording the shit?" "Ay yo, Reggie, what the fuck are you doing? turn that shit off". Toni tries to push my arm out the way so she can get closer to Edira's face ...big mistake. Edira mushed the shit out of Toni and they began to tussle on the floor. I got in the middle of them and tried to break it up. These bitches are strong. I managed to get them separated and Toni goes for the steak knife on the counter. I jumped in front of Edira. "Toni you need to calm the fuck down. what the fuck is going on wit y'all?" Toni said, "what's wrong with me... what's wrong with me? I'll tell you what's wrong with me. I entered this relationship doing what I needed to do, so that you and I could be a family. I didn't want this, I just wanted you. But, I had to play the fucking part so that you would fall for me and not want her."

"Wait what? Why would you think I didn't want her? She's my Michelle, the first lady, Bitch."

"If you wanted her, then you wouldn't of been looking for me, nigga."

"We would've been on baby number 2 but I just wasn't ready."

"What? You were pregnant before? Wait, you're pregnant now? What the fuck?"

"Yes, I'm pregnant again and I'm keeping it."

At this point, Toni is out of breath, but still holding the knife. Edira yells 'put the knife down so I can finish whooping your ass."

"Naw, you can't fight her, Edira, she's pregnant."

Edira looks Eric in his face, "two can play that game," and tosses her ultrasound on the kitchen floor. Reggie's mouth is wide open, looking just as crazy as everyone in the house at this point.

Toni looks down at the black and white sonogram and screams, "you old bitch. I knew I should of OD your ass!!!" And she charges toward Edira with the knife.

Eric grabs Toni and slices his hand. He yells at the top of his lungs. "You cut me Toni! You fucking cut me!!!!." At this point Reggie is on the phone with 911 yelling in the phone "these crazy bitches got my man sliced and diced, y'all need to hurry the fuck up." The police arrive not even 7 minutes later with guns drawn. Toni drops the knife and they begin to put her in hand cuffs. The ambulance pulls up and then another squad car right behind it. The medics rush to the front porch to check on Eric.

Then this shapely officer who was wearing regular clothes came up to the porch frantic. "Baby, are you ok? Eric, what happened?"

"Baby? Baby?" Edira and Toni look at Eric. "Who's she calling baby?"

Tiana stepped back and said, "I'm calling my man baby. Is there a problem?"

"Oh hell naw." Reggie said. "You about to be in a fatal attraction in this, bitch."

Edira looks at Eric and then at Tiana and then towards the squad car where the officer was walking Toni to. Edira's eyes well up with tears. "I was never enough!! I was never enough!! This is the life I choose to live, but your selfish ass couldn't get enough!"

Tiana steps back and crosses her arms over each other and begins to shake her head. "Wow, Eric! Wow! I thought you were different, but you're no better than Xavier! How dare you!!!" All of a sudden… *pop pop pop*… and a loud scream. Tiana falls to the ground. They tackled the gun from Toni and force her into the squad car. Edira is still in shock but feels a burning sensation near her abdomen and everything goes dark.

EPILOGUE

EDIRA

1 year and half later I'm driving in the car listening to my music. I glance up at the rearview mirror at Ethan Amari. Ethan Amari meaning Strong and gift from God. When I woke up from emergency surgery I knew I had lost the baby and did; but what I didn't know was I was pregnant with twins. The baby I lost saved Ethan. Eric stayed at the hospital until the doctor told him he had to leave to give his statement to the police, so all he knew was the baby didn't make it. The Nurse was on her way out to the waiting room to let him know that the other baby would survive but he was gone already. Once I was ok to leave from the hospital I left everything that had to do with that relationship there. I never spoke to Eric again. I felt like his way of living almost took mine.

"This Woman's Work" by Maxwell starts playing on the radio and then my cell phone rings. I don't recognize the number but I decided to answer it anyways. It was Eric he sounded upset and hurt. He called to tell me that he got a call from the prison that Toni had taken her life and that she left him to take care of their daughter. All I could do was feel bad for him. He lost me, he lost Toni and apparently he had a loss for words.

I asked him to let me know the arrangements because even though Toni was crazy she had a baby that was my son's sister. I prepared myself for the services and went to pay my respects. There was a good amount of people still at the church entrance, but I could only see Eric. Eric walked over to my car where my mom was bouncing my son. Eric just looked and said, "you got a handsome little fella there."

I said, "thank you, he takes after his daddy."

He said, "he must be a good-looking man."

I said, "maybe I'll ask him." I reached into the car and introduced my son to his father. Eric was shocked. He looked at me then looked at my son and burst into tears. "Hey little man, hey I'm your daddy." He gripped and cuddled Ethan like he would never see him again. Once the services were over he asked if he could go to a park with me and bring his daughter. I agreed and we made plans for the following day. Eric walked into the park area holding the cutest little brown baby I've ever seen. She was the perfect combination of Eric and Toni. He asked me how I'd been. I told him I was doing ok. Then we reminisced about the good old times for a minute. He told me he received some letters from Toni before her passing and had one that was addressed to me. I had a little uncertainty but took the letter and decided to read it.

Dear Edira: I'm Sorry... I never meant to hurt you... I was blinded by love. I sacrificed my freedom for a man that really only loved you. I believe he was feeding his ego but I knew he was deep in love with you. I overheard him one night on the phone telling someone that you were everything he could ever ask for and that he had been a fool to want more, but his selfishness got the best of him. I know you don't believe me, but you were like a big sister and confidante to me and I will forever appreciate the wisdom you shed upon me. I was intimidated by your strength and Power and let my lack of confidence put me in a negative space. You will forever be a Pilar of guidance in my life and I hope that you continue to be the boss bitch that you've always been. I hope that this letter reaches you in good health and I pray that you will help Eric take care of my baby girl. Her name is Edira Evlyne. She will be a beautiful soul without me because that's the life I choose to live.

ABOUT THE AUTHOR

Jasmin Brown was Born and raised in the City of Champions, Brockton Massachusetts. Jasmin graduated with a degree in Social Science.

Jasmin is the mother of two beautiful little girls, Victoria and Jayanii. Through trying obstacles, Jasmin has overcome many barriers and continues to stay focused through life's trials and tribulations. Her greatest achievements are her girls and advocating for her youngest daughter who suffers from a Hearing Disability.

Jasmin works as a Program Coordinator helping young adults with limitations to find employment. She hopes that you enjoy this short story and if you have dreams and aspirations to never give up, because you have a purpose.

Jasmin has been on the cover of two books written by her sister Kenya Brown-Milfort. Jasmin's goal in life is to continue to strive for Happiness.

CPSIA information can be obtained
at www.ICGtesting.com
Printed in the USA
FSHW022153110421